For friend, writer and polar bear whizz David Bedford,
and Kate, Isobel and Tom - P.L.

For all polar bears and the people who work to protect them - G.H.

First published in Great Britain in 2008
by Piccadilly Press Ltd,
5 Castle Road, London NW1 8PR
www.piccadillypress.co.uk

Designed by Simon Davis
Printed and bound by WKT in China
Colour reproduction by Dot Gradations

ISBN: 978 1 85340 962 2 (hardback)

ISBN: 978 1 85340 961 5 (paperback)

3 5 7 9 10 8 6 4 2

A catalogue record of this book is available from the British Library

Best Friends Or Not?

Paeony Lewis • Gaby Hansen

PICCADILLY PRESS • LONDON

Nanook and Suka were best friends.

They always played snowballs together.

But sometimes Nanook didn't want to play snowballs. Instead, he wanted to climb the ice peak and whizz down.

Suka didn't.

Nanook wanted to swim from
iceberg to iceberg.

Suka didn't.

Nanook wanted to play explorers
in the ice cave.

Suka didn't.

Suka ONLY wanted to throw snowballs.

"We NEVER play what
I want to play," said Nanook.
"It's not fair!"

Splat!
Suka's snowball
hit Nanook
on the nose.

That's when Nanook
and Suka stopped
being best friends.

Without Suka, Nanook climbed the ice peak that Suka wouldn't climb.

He was as high as the birds. "Hello gulls," called Nanook.

Then Nanook whizzed down.
Wheeee!

Nanook splashed into the sea.
"Hello seals," he said.

They all swam to the icebergs, where Suka wouldn't go, and played chase until it was time for the seals to have their nap.

Nanook waved goodbye to
the sleepy seals. "I'll do some
exploring on my own," he said.

Slowly, Nanook crept into
the mysterious ice cave
that Suka wouldn't explore.

Deep inside,
something
sparkled.
There were
hundreds
of icicles!

Nanook wished
Suka could
see them
too.

DING DANG DONG!
Nanook played musical icicles.
And soon he wasn't alone.

Two Arctic fox cubs stopped and sang to his twinkling music before going on their way.

Outside the cave, it had begun to snow.
Nanook stood alone and watched the falling
snowflakes. Gusts of wind swirled them into shapes.

"Dancing snowbears,"
whispered
Nanook.

Nanook danced.
He danced with his
silent snow friends.

Too soon, the sun came out and the snowflakes drifted away. So Nanook decided to make his own snow friend.

He piled up snow.

He patted it into shape.
But it didn't look right.

"What are you making?" whispered a voice.

Nanook turned and saw . . .

Suka!

"I'm trying to build a snowbear," said Nanook.

Suka smiled shyly and asked, "Can I help?"
"I thought you only wanted to play snowballs," said Nanook.

“It’s no fun on my own,” said Suka. “I missed you.”
“I missed you too,” said Nanook.
Together, Suka and Nanook
built a snowbear.

“That was almost as fun as snowballs,” said Suka.
“Now what shall we play?”

"Let's race
down the ice peak,"
suggested Nanook.
"Whoever wins gets to choose the next game.
That's fair."
Suka grinned and, as fast as they could, they
climbed the ice peak and whizzed down.

Nanook won!
"So what do we play next?" asked Suka.
Nanook thought and then he said . . .

"I want to play snowballs with my best friend!"

And that's what they did!